LISA: BOOK THREE

THE TROUBLE WITH GOLD

PRISCILLA GALLOWAY

NT

**Look for the other Lisa stories
in Our Canadian Girl**

Book One: Overland to Cariboo

Book Two: The Trail to Golden Cariboo

LISA: BOOK THREE
THE TROUBLE WITH GOLD
PRISCILLA GALLOWAY

PENGUIN
CANADA

PENGUIN CANADA

Published by the Penguin Group

Penguin Group (Canada), 90 Eglinton Avenue East, Suite 700, Toronto, Ontario, Canada M4P 2Y3
(a division of Pearson Canada Inc.)

Penguin Group (USA) Inc., 375 Hudson Street, New York, New York 10014, U.S.A.
Penguin Books Ltd, 80 Strand, London WC2R 0RL, England
Penguin Ireland, 25 St Stephen's Green, Dublin 2, Ireland (a division of Penguin Books Ltd)
Penguin Group (Australia), 250 Camberwell Road, Camberwell, Victoria 3124, Australia
(a division of Pearson Australia Group Pty Ltd)
Penguin Books India Pvt Ltd, 11 Community Centre, Panchsheel Park, New Delhi – 110 017, India
Penguin Group (NZ), cnr Airborne and Rosedale Roads, Albany, Auckland 1310, New Zealand
(a division of Pearson New Zealand Ltd)
Penguin Books (South Africa) (Pty) Ltd, 24 Sturdee Avenue, Rosebank, Johannesburg 2196,
South Africa

Penguin Books Ltd, Registered Offices: 80 Strand, London WC2R 0RL, England

First published 2006

1 2 3 4 5 6 7 8 9 10 (WEB)

Copyright © Priscilla Galloway, 2006
Illustrations copyright © Don Kilby, 2006
Design: Matthews Communications Design Inc.
Map copyright © Sharon Matthews

Manufactured in Canada.

LIBRARY AND ARCHIVES CANADA CATALOGUING IN PUBLICATION

Galloway, Priscilla, 1930–
Lisa, book three : the trouble with gold / Priscilla Galloway.

(Our Canadian girl)
ISBN-13: 978-0-14-305012-4
ISBN-10: 0-14-305012-5

1. Cariboo (B.C. : Regional district)—Gold discoveries—Juvenile fiction.
I. Title. II. Title: Trouble with gold. III. Series.

PS8563.A45L568 2006   jC813'.54   C2005-907767-0

Visit the Penguin Group (Canada) website at **www.penguin.ca**

Special and corporate bulk purchase rates available; please see
www.penguin.ca/corporatesales or call 1-800-399-6858, ext. 477 or 474

With love to my grandmother
Angusta Peebles, née Grant, 1865–1955

Be good, sweet maid, and let who will be clever;

Do noble deeds, not dream them all day long,

And so make life, death, and that vast forever

One grand, sweet song.

William Cullen Bryant

My grandmother wrote this stanza in my autograph book when I was Lisa's age. I understood her message, but I resented it mightily. Not that I objected to goodness—indeed, I was generally in favour of it. However, the little poem reminded me cruelly that I could never manage to be "good" for very long, and nobody ever described me as "sweet." Cleverness was much more my style, and it was a shame that my grandmother did not seem to value it. Besides, surely I had to be clever to think of noble deeds to do; and daydreaming about noble deeds would help in planning them. Grandma had chosen badly for me. Maybe she had me mixed up with one of my sisters.

However, maybe Grandma was not thinking at all about what kind of person I was. She probably agreed with the ideas in the poem and admired the way the poet expressed them. Grandma was born in 1865, only two years later than the time of Lisa's story.

I still dislike the poem, but I have spent many hours considering it over the years. Reluctant though I am to admit it, those lines have given me insight into myself and a goal to strive for. For four lines of not-very-good Victorian verse, that's quite an achievement, and it's the reason this book is dedicated, with love, to my grandmother Angusta Peebles, née Grant, 1865–1955.

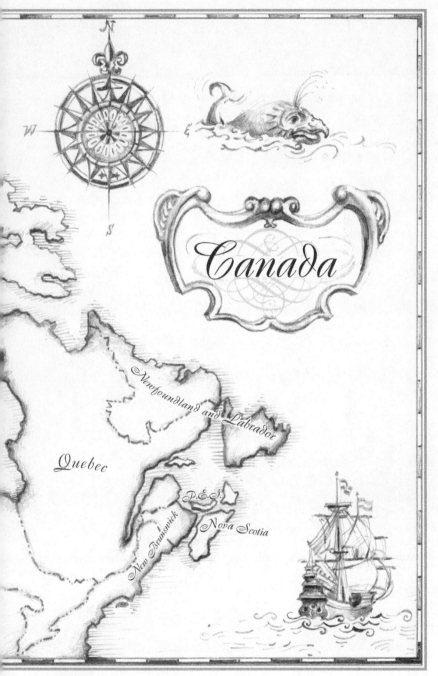

Canada

Quebec

Newfoundland and Labrador

New Brunswick

P.E.I.

Nova Scotia

 Marks the location of the story

GOLD FEVER

TEN-YEAR-OLD LISA SCHUBERT has crossed prairies, swamps, and mountains; rafted down a wild river; saved herself and her brother from drowning; and helped when a baby was born. All this happened during the five months she spent travelling with her family—and almost 200 men—from Fort Garry (now Winnipeg), to Kamloops in present-day British Columbia.

The Overlanders, including Lisa, had set out to make their fortunes in the Cariboo gold rush. When fellow Overlander Archibald McNaughton invited Lisa to go north to the gold rush towns with him and his bride, it seemed her prayers had been answered. Lisa was certain that she would be able to go gold mining with Archie and his partners.

While travelling to the Cariboo, Lisa was almost pushed off a cliff by unruly camels! Instead, she saved Mrs. Mac's horse, winning the bride's gratitude and the opportunity to ride—if she had owned the right kind of clothes and been able to ride sidesaddle.

In Cameronton, where Archie and his partners had staked their claims and Archie had built his modest home, Lisa headed for the site of the future mine. She wasn't allowed to go underground, so she took a pickaxe and furiously bashed the rocks that had been dug out from the shaft. They split apart, exposing the buttery sheen of a gold nugget. On her very first visit to the property, Lisa had found gold! A miner could hardly have made a better start. However, Lisa's luck did not continue.

What kind of life might a real-life Lisa have experienced at the height of the Cariboo gold rush? Cameronton in the summer of 1863 was a town full of strangers, almost all of them men, with more trudging in every day. They hoped to make a fortune and take their riches somewhere else; indeed, most of them would go south for the winter, which was long and harsh throughout the region.

The Cariboo was Canada's first major gold rush. Compared with the California gold rush, ten years earlier in the United States, and the Klondike rush, thirty-five years later (1897–1900), it was not huge. Few men made fortunes; fewer still kept them. Men who struck it rich seemed to believe that there would always be more. In fact, nobody ever did find the fabled "mother lode," that vast seam of gold from which many prospectors believed that the nuggets in the rivers had come. There was no mother lode in the Cariboo.

The gold was there, but it was dispersed and therefore difficult and expensive to recover. Individual miners were soon bought out by big companies with enough money to bring a mine into production, but that came later than Lisa's story.

The gold rush was a short-lived phenomenon. The boom lasted little more than five years, though some mining continued for six decades afterward. All the towns eventually died. Only Barkerville still exists, and it has been restored as a heritage tourist site; it is not a place where people live and work.

If Lisa had been there, she would not have found friends her own age. Few women braved the cruel weather and frontier rudeness of life in the Cariboo in those early days. Only a handful of women had stayed through the previous winter.

Lisa's strong character was the product of an unusual life. In the ordinary course of events, a child of her age would have had less freedom and independence. I have presented Lisa as unusual for her time and her actions as shocking to some adults. That would have been true.

Occasionally, I have telescoped some events that were, in fact, spread over a longer time than in my book. However, all significant events in this story are firmly based in history, including Cariboo Cameron's big party and Eliza Ord's shameful treatment, which illustrates all too well the obstacles faced by a single woman who wanted to be a miner. Women then were not treated the same as men under the law, and men did not welcome female competition. (Women were not legally "persons" in Canada until 1929!)

Deprived of other female companionship, the miners welcomed the dancing partners imported by an enterprising saloon owner. The Hurdy Gurdies took their name from the instrument that often provided their music. One photo of several Hurdy Gurdies has survived, showing them on the porch of the hotel in their gigantic hooped skirts.

Hoops had become wider and wider, until a woman dressed in her best might have trouble passing through a door. In the fashion capitals of the world, hoops would soon be replaced by bustles, but the new styles would not arrive in outposts like the Cariboo for several years. The hoops were sewn to a long petticoat, often four hoops, gradually getting larger toward the bottom. This gave a bell effect to the skirt draped over them. A child could easily hide under a fashionable mother's skirts!

In this story, Lisa takes refuge behind, not underneath, some enormous hooped skirts. These Hurdy Gurdies protect her from her enemy, the villainous Samuel Stokes. Mr. Stokes wants Lisa's gold nugget! Will she be able to keep it and use it to help her family, as she has planned?

CHAPTER N⁰ 1

Dear Ma and Papa, Gus, Mary Jane, Jamie, and
Baby Rose,

    *I am the luckiest miner in the Cariboo. Mr. Wattie
says so and Archie—Mr. McNaughton—and even
Cariboo Cameron his very own self! He has not long
been back from burying his wife in Victoria.
Cameronton, where Archie has built his house, is
named after Cariboo Cameron, because he found so
much gold.*

    Why am I so lucky?

    *Archie took me and Mrs. McNaughton out to his
diggings yesterday—and I found a gold nugget!*

I bashed some rocks with a pickaxe—Archie and his partners had dug them up—and there it was. Papa, it's enough money for you to buy a horse and cart and send for my trunk from Fort Garry—only I can't send the gold to you with this letter because it might get lost or stolen even.

My nugget will be safe here until you come. Mr. Wattie is one of Archie's partners—you remember he showed Archie and me how to pan for gold. We don't pan for gold here in the Cariboo. We have to dig deep holes and put logs around so the dirt won't fall on top of us and then we climb down a ladder.

I haven't climbed down yet. Mrs. McNaughton said ladies don't climb down ladders, and ladies don't go mining, but then I found my nugget, and now Mr. Wattie says I should climb down the ladder and bring them luck, so I guess she will change her mind. But maybe she won't. She is very set in her ways.

Papa, when you come to the Cariboo, we can find gold together. I expect I am lucky enough for both of us. *Mrs. McNaughton gave me this paper to write on and she let me use her pen and ink. Sorry about all the inkblots—this pen is scratchy.*

   Lovingly yours,
   Lisa

"Are you finished writing your letter?" Mrs. Mac asked. "Let me read it over, Lisa, and check your spelling."

Oh my goodness; she would see what I'd said! When I was writing, I had pretended my family was right there, Ma and Papa and the children, and I was talking to them, but not Mrs. Mac—I was not talking to her! "Please, ma'am, don't trouble yourself," I told her. I could feel my face getting red.

Mrs. Mac was very strong on duty. I was sure she was going to tell me it was her duty to correct my spelling. Then she would hold out her hand and wait, and I would have to give her my letter. But she didn't. She looked at me for quite a long time, and then she sighed. "Very well, not this time," she said. "Have you left any space to write Mr. Schubert's name?"

"No, ma'am," I said. I had covered every inch of the paper, both sides. My writing kept getting smaller so I could squeeze everything in.

"Never mind," she said. "I will write a note to go with it."

"Who will take my letter?" I asked her.

"Barnard's Express, I think," she replied. "Maybe they won't take it all the way to Kamloops, though."

The door opened and Archie walked in. "You are early for dinner, Mr. McNaughton." His wife smiled. "It's not yet noon. Lisa, set the table, please."

"Not yet," said Archie. "Lisa, I must ask you to go to your room. Mrs. McNaughton and I have private matters to discuss."

I hate it when grown-ups shut me out. It's mean. I started up the narrow stairs as slowly as I could. I was only halfway up when someone pounded on the front door. I turned as it swung open. A skinny little runt of a man stepped inside. He was dressed like a miner: red flannel shirt, heavy pants, and all. A fierce man, for all his small size; his black beard bristled up the sides of his face to join his long black hair. His jaws moved up and down; the chewing motion seemed angry too.

"So, where's this nugget?" he demanded. "The first real money on our land and you give it away? What kind of a partner are you anyway, Archibald McNaughton?"

"Calm down, Samuel," Archie said. "I've just this minute come home. I must think what's best to do."

The little man stared at Mrs. Mac, then at me. Mrs. Mac glided over to her husband, her grey hooped skirt swaying around her feet. She put her hand on Archie's arm. "Mr. McNaughton," she said, "pray introduce this gentleman. Your partner, I think he said?"

"Samuel Stokes, ma'am," the man replied. "At your service, ma'am, I suppose." His jaws had stopped moving, but his cheek was full. Chewing tobacco, no doubt. Mrs. Mac called it a filthy habit, and I agreed with her.

"Best be on your way now and come back later, Samuel," said Archie. "Give me an hour or two."

Samuel Stokes glared up at me. He didn't move. "It don't need no thinking about," he said. He sucked in his cheeks and spat, deliberately, in my direction. "You've got gold that belongs to me and my partners, little missy," he said. "Begging your pardon, ma'am," he nodded toward Mrs. Mac, "but I'm here for what's mine."

"I'll thank you to leave at once, Mr. Stokes, as my husband requested." Mrs. Mac's voice was as cold as ice. "Partner or not, you are not welcome in my home."

She faced him, standing like the picture of our Queen Victoria in the schoolroom back at Fort Garry. The little man's shoulders drooped. He slunk toward the door, muttering something I couldn't hear to Archie as he passed.

"You've got gold that belongs to me and my partners, little missy," he said. "Begging your pardon, ma'am," he nodded toward Mrs. Mac, "but I'm here for what's mine."

"My nugget?" I asked uncertainly. "It isn't his. How could it be? *I* found it. It was in that rock pile. Archie—Mrs. McNaughton—I found it, didn't I?"

"That you did, Lisa," Mrs. Mac replied.

Mr. Stokes swung round to face me again, his back to the door. "I'll go, but I'll be back." He sucked in his cheeks as if to spit again, then glanced at Mrs. Mac and thought better of it. He glared at me. "Whose land were you standing on? Whose rock pile was that? Whose pickaxe did you use to split that rock? Think about that, girlie. I'll be back." The door slammed behind him.

Mrs. Mac held out her arms and I stumbled into them. Her corsets were still as stiff as when I'd saved her horse, Queenie, from tumbling over a precipice, but her arms were strong. She patted my shoulder.

I shivered. Just when everything is going right, that's when things go wrong; I can count on it. "I want my family," I gulped. "I want Ma and Papa and Jamie and Baby Rose and Mary Jane and Gus, even if he teases me. Oh, Archie, can't I keep my nugget?"

"He's partly right," said Archie. "You did find it on our claim. I came home early to talk to my wife about this, Lisa. Now I think you should join us."

Yesterday, I had wanted to run around and tell everybody, "I found gold. I'm a miner. I'm rich." Last night, though, I woke up and wondered. Maybe one nugget was not enough to make me rich or to look after my family. Now a man named Samuel Stokes wanted to take even that one nugget away from me.

We sat around the table. A heavy damask cloth, already showing stains I could not scrub out of its white surface, covered the rough planks.

"It's like this," said Archie. "Me and my partners, we each staked one claim. A claim is a hundred feet wide. If it's on a river, it goes back quite a piece. Our claims aren't right on the creek, but they're shaped the same, next to each other. Seven hundred feet."

"I thought you told me there were five men in your company," said Mrs. Mac. "But you each staked one claim. Are there seven of you then?"

"Not now," said Archie. "There were seven of us to start with, but two of them ran out of money and grub. They sold out to James Wattie and me, so we have two shares each, and the other three own one apiece. We don't have much cash money left, Lisa."

"Nobody said anything yesterday, when Lisa found her nugget," said Mrs. Mac quietly.

"No," Archie agreed. "James Wattie was there, but the others didn't hear about it until later, and the news was all around town by then. Samuel has been steaming for a good few hours."

I just looked at Archie. My dream was slipping away. "Even if you let me go mining with you," I said, "even if I find more gold, it belongs to you and your partners, is that it?" My voice quavered.

"That's it," said Archie.

My rock, with the nugget sticking out, weighed down my pocket. I took it out and stroked it, admiring its golden sheen. "I found it," I said. "You threw it away."

"Not exactly," said Archie. "We run all rock through the crusher. If there's any gold in a pile, we'll find it. You just found this piece sooner. James Wattie is a good man, Lisa. He says you've brought us luck and you should keep that nugget. There'll be more where it came from, he says. I expect he's right, but it's the first gold we've found, and we've been digging on this shaft for three long months. You can maybe see where Samuel is disappointed. He wants us partners to sell this gold and share out the money." He sighed.

"So here we are, arguing when we should be digging like crazy. James Wattie is out at the mine with the others. I hope they're digging, but maybe they're just talking." He leaned his head on his hands. "James and I say you should have the nugget, Lisa. That's four votes out of seven— but you see how Samuel feels; it's like enough the other two will agree with him."

"That will make bad feeling among all of you," said Mrs. Mac quietly.

Maybe it's easier when you don't find gold; that way you don't have to fight over it. However, I knew what Ma would do if she were here. I stroked the soft, shining metal and then pushed the nugget over to Archie. "Take it," I said. "Share it with your partners."

"That's generous indeed, Lisa," said Archie.

"Don't do it," said Mrs. Mac indignantly. "You are not the Lord, Mr. McNaughton, to take away what is given."

"That I am not," Archie agreed. He pushed the nugget back in my direction. "This can wait," he said. "I'd best get back to the mine, try to mend fences with the others, and not give Sam more time to turn them against James Wattie and me."

"Are you not hungry?" said Mrs. Mac. "I would be failing in my duty if you do not stop to eat dinner before you go. Please sit, my dear. You too, Lisa."

We sat and ate slices of beef cut from Saturday's roast and heated in gravy, beans again—Mrs. Mac hoped to buy some potatoes soon, for variety— and a dish of onions with a butter sauce. It was a good dinner, better than most we had on the trail, but I didn't really enjoy it, nor, from their grim faces, did Archie and Mrs. Mac. I felt calmer, though, when Archie set down his knife and fork and wiped his mouth. "Excellent, dear Elizabeth," he said, as he folded his big white napkin and slid it into a massive silver ring engraved with his initials. Mrs. Mac and I too folded our napkins; Mrs. Mac walked with Archie to the door.

Then she turned to me. "I'll pour water for the dishes," she said, "then I think we will go out, Lisa. We must begin to be acquainted with this town."

I washed the dishes. Mrs. Mac dried them with a soft cloth and set the room to rights. We tied our bonnets; Mrs. Mac smoothed on a soft pair of white kid gloves. It was a marvel to me how she kept them clean. I was thankful indeed that she did not expect me to wear gloves, except, of course, for Sunday services.

Mrs. Mac opened the door, stepped out, and tripped on the stoop, falling in a flurry of hoops and petticoats. She gasped; I was the one who screamed. No neighbours came running, though. Houses lined the street, but it seemed no one was home. Mrs. Mac's gloves were filthy with dust and mud. That shocked me, her white gloves ruined. In the moment, that's what I thought of, not that she herself must be hurt. "Get up, ma'am, let me help you." I tugged at her hands.

"One minute, child," she gasped. "Let me catch my breath." She breathed heavily, in great gulps. Then she steadied herself against the door frame on one side and my shoulder on the other and slowly levered herself up. She stepped away from the entrance and pulled her skirts back out of the way.

"I tripped over something," she said quietly. We both stared. On the step lay the unmoving body of a raccoon, a small one, clown mask turned up to the sky. Mrs. Mac stepped toward it and then stopped with a grimace of pain.

"Come inside, ma'am," I said. "I'll run and fetch your husband." I took her arm as she gingerly stepped over the raccoon and back inside.

"You should not go by yourself," she said, "but there's not much choice. We do need help. Mr. McNaughton won't expect to come home much before dark." She paused. I steadied her as she sat down again in her rough chair. She put her arms on the table, her elbows too, though she was forever at me to take mine off it.

"Go quickly, Lisa," she said, "but watch where you put your feet."

"I'm glad I don't wear hooped skirts," I said.

"Hmph!" Mrs. Mac snorted; then she laughed. "Be off with you," she said.

CHAPTER 2

Despite Mrs. Mac's advice, I started running as fast as I could, slowing down only when I tripped over a piece of rusty iron, likely from some abandoned piece of mining machinery. I almost fell, but didn't, and went on slowly, paying heed.

Now too I began thinking. How had a dead raccoon got to our stoop? Someone must have put it there. It could hardly have happened by chance. Now who could that someone be?

Samuel Stokes came instantly to mind, angry Samuel. When I heard his threatening voice

behind me, it was almost as if I had been expect-
ing him. "Judge Begbie is coming to town,
girlie," the voice said. "The hanging judge, they
call him. He don't care for high-graders and
claim jumpers and such. I'll sue for what's mine,
and the hanging judge will take a long hard look
at that pretty white neck of yours." He snickered,
a horrid sound.

"Go away," I said, trying to sound brave. "You
can't scare me."

Judge Begbie wouldn't hang a child, would he?
Mr. Wattie had given me the nugget—if it was his
to give. My voice trembled, though. Where could
I run?

I looked around wildly. The Occidental Hotel
was closest, and I could see some ladies sitting on
the front verandah. As I ran up the path, I saw
that they were all dressed in the same red muslin
shirtwaists and dark printed skirts, with their hair
up in some kind of topknot under their little red
caps. Their skirts spread way out on both sides;
they had to be wearing the most enormous

hoops I had ever seen. My feet carried me in a final burst of speed up the stairs. I jumped between two of the ladies' skirts. Samuel Stokes stood in the road, rocking back and forth, from heels to toes, then back again. "Hello, ladies," he said. When he smiled, he showed all his teeth.

One of the women beckoned to him. "Comen here," she called. I wondered if she was German. She sounded just like Papa—Mr. Schubert, that is. She talked like he used to, before he got used to English.

Mr. Stokes laughed. "Later, Fraulein Greta," he said. "I'll come to the saloon." He waved cheerfully before he turned his back and sauntered down the road, heading back to town.

Shivering, I backed away from the lady he had talked to. My road to Archie was, for the moment, clear.

"Thank you," I said. "I'll go now."

The ladies looked at me. They weren't shocked, I could see that, but they were curious. "What was that about?" one of them asked. Her

English was easy to understand. "Child, you're shaking. Don't go yet." She pulled out a tiny silver flask from her bosom and unstoppered it. She waved it under my nose. "Here, sniff," she said.

I guessed what it was, but not before I had taken a deep breath. Smelling salts! I coughed and coughed. My eyes watered, but I didn't feel tired or dizzy any more. Were they friends with Mr. Stokes? How could I find out?

"You're from Germany," I gulped when I could talk again.

"Straight from Baden-Baden," said the lady proudly. "Though I lived in San Francisco for a while. How did you guess?"

Now I laughed, a little. Samuel Stokes had said Fraulein, not Miss or Madam. "Fraulein Greta talks like *mein* papa," I said, throwing in two of my few German words. Two of the ladies began talking at once in a flood of German. I shook my head. *"Nein,"* I said. *"Nein sprechen.* I speak English."

"They don't," said the smelling salts lady. "English I learned in California. Pretty good, huh?"

"Yes," I agreed. "Mr. Stokes scared me. I don't like him."

"He's rich man," said Fraulein Greta.

What could I say? I shook my head. Maybe I didn't understand her. Then I remembered Mrs. Mac, sitting at home with her hurt leg. How could I have forgotten, even for a minute? "I have to go." I raced down the stairs. "I'll come back later," I called back over my shoulder. "Thank you." All of them waved as I hurried on my way.

CHAPTER *N°* 3

At the mine, two men stood beside the open shaft, hauling up a bucket full of rock and dirt, bluish stuff, heavy like clay. One man picked up an empty bucket; the other hoisted the full one, ready to dump it on the stone pile. The pickaxe still leaned against the rocks, where I had put it yesterday.

I didn't know these men, but I knew I'd better take time to be friendly. They had to be the other partners. James Wattie and Archie were likely down in the tunnel.

"I'm Lisa," I said. "I hope you aren't mad at

me, like Mr. Stokes."

A long rope dangled from a pulley that hung from the tripod of logs over the dark circle of the shaft, the entrance to the mine. The man with the wooden bucket laughed as he tied the rope around its handle. The bucket clunked against the side of the shaft as he lowered it. "I'm David Ross," he said. "Archie says you want to be a miner."

"I do," I said.

"A female don't do no good on her own," Mr. Ross said. "Anybody will tell you the same. But a young female, now, one that could cut her hair short and wear a cap like a boy, ready to crawl into cracks that's too tight for a man, one that's not afraid of the dark, she might do just fine. Especially if she has friends. Do you know anybody like that?" He winked a bright blue eye.

"You're trying to scare me." I tried to sound as if it wasn't working. Dark cracks too tight for a man? "I want to find gold; I know I can."

"You're crazy," said the other man, coming back with his empty bucket. "You're as crazy as that female that got sent away to the madhouse in New Westminster. What was her name now? Eliza something? You couldn't even crank the windlass when we build one and pull up a full bucket. You're too small. A mine is no place for a girl. Go home where you belong."

"This here's Adam Bailey," said Mr. Ross. "He's usually a quiet man. He's not in the habit of being rude to a young lady. Isn't that right, Adam?"

"Hmph," Mr. Bailey grumbled.

"If you please, sir," I said, trembling again, "Mrs. McNaughton has been injured. I came here to fetch her husband." I bent over the shaft and yelled for Archie. Who cared if I sounded like a lady or not? Mr. Ross grabbed my shoulders and pulled me roughly back from the dark hole.

Archie's white face appeared suddenly out of the blackness as he climbed quickly up the ladder. "What did you say? She's hurt? How bad,

Lisa? Oh Lord, and we have no doctor, not until we build the hospital, and we won't even turn the sod for another three weeks."

I glared at Mr. Ross, even though anybody could see he had been scared I'd fall down the shaft. "I think she is not bad," I said to Archie. "She tripped on a dead animal and fell, just outside the door. I should have stayed to bind up her leg, but she sent me off to fetch you, and everything else went clean out of my head."

James Wattie followed Archie out of the shaft. "I heard all that," he said. "Off you go, Archie. Don't come in tomorrow if your wife is poorly. If you need help, Jennie Allen and Johanna Maguire are good nurses."

"I'm a good nurse too," I said. "I helped birth my sister, Baby Rose, and I've cared for all the children when they were ill." Archie's long legs had already carried him far down the road. I had to run to catch up.

Archie fussed over her, but Mrs. Mac laughed at him, though she was content to keep her leg up on a pillow covering the seat of our fourth chair. She was a funny sight, with her hoops up and her pantaloons and petticoats showing. I tried not to laugh, as I bound her ankle with a long strip of flannel, but a fit of the giggles took me, and I couldn't stop. She saw the funny side and laughed too, though not in her usual hearty fashion.

"Women," said Archie in disgust, "I'll never understand 'em. Surely you should be in your bed, my love." He looked down at her, then quickly bent and gathered her into his arms, hoops, petticoats, and all.

"Mr. McNaughton, really!" she protested but not as if she meant it.

"Mrs. McNaughton, really," he quietly replied.

The next morning, Mrs. Mac was up early, as usual. I had promised myself I'd be up first and start a fire in the stove, but I overslept. The fragrant smell of coffee drifted up to my room and woke me pleasantly. I washed and dressed and hurried down to find Archie and Mrs. Mac with their plates empty and their cups well on the way to being empty as well.

"Stop dawdling over your coffee and get along with you, Mr. McNaughton," said Mrs. Mac, smiling. "I won't need you; but if for some reason I do, Lisa can run and fetch you again, can't you?"

"Of course," I said. The sun shone warm and bright. I felt safe and happy. I wanted nothing to spoil that feeling, so I did not tell them about Samuel Stokes's nasty behaviour the previous day or about the women on the verandah at the Occidental Hotel. I did not ask about the madwoman, Eliza whatever-her-name-might-be.

I was full of energy. I carried water from the creek and put it to boil for drinking. I made bread dough and kneaded it, then set three loaves to rise. I took all the dishes out of the cupboards and dusted the shelves. I swept the floors. I heated water and did the laundry, though there wasn't much. I even went out and pulled weeds from the garden, hoping it was the weeds I was pulling and not new little plants. In between all these tasks, I made tea and fetched Mrs. Mac's writing desk so that she could set it on her knees and write letters to her friends in Montreal.

By early afternoon the bread was in the oven, and I could not find anything more to do. "You'd better go to the store and buy me some more writing paper," said Mrs. Mac. "You're full of the fidgets, Lisa. It makes me tired just watching you. Bring me my purse."

I brought her sealskin purse. The brown fur was stitched to a top made of engraved silver, and the clasp slid back and forth and locked with a key. She gave me money for the writing paper. "Good quality rag paper, mind," she told me. I twisted the coins into an old handkerchief and put them in my pocket.

"Will you be all right?" I asked. "Won't Mr. McNaughton be cross if I leave you alone?"

"Not when you've gone on an errand for me," she said firmly. "Stay out of mischief, Lisa, but you need not hurry back. I am going to have a nap."

The dirt road was grooved by wagon wheels. I walked on the side, my skirts brushing against tall grass and weeds, careful to stay clear of the horse dung, especially the fresh droppings that steamed here and there. I passed two small log houses, both smaller than Archie's, and one tent, erected on a foundation of logs, with a chimney pipe sticking up at the back. Then the businesses began.

First was the Cameron & Ames Blacksmith shop. Heat blasted from the open shed at the side, where the smith held the leg of a chestnut pony under one massive arm while he hammered a new shoe on her hoof with the other. I gawped for a minute or two. The smith shook sweat from his face, saw me, and smiled. I waved and went on. Next was F. J. Barnard's Express, with three horses tethered in front. Barnard's had carried my letter home. Would they have brought a letter for me? I could see the sign for the post office next door, past an empty lot, so I went in and asked, for me and for the McNaughtons.

"Nothing today," said the postmaster, "but try again day after tomorrow." He did not sell writing paper, but he showed me two pink postage stamps, with Queen Victoria's face in black, one for two pence and the other for a half-penny. "They are new," he said. "You have to stick them on. Soon everybody will buy stamps when they send a letter." I wondered if Archie had bought stamps when he sent my letter to my family. How much did he have to pay?

As I turned to go, the postmaster said, "Wait a minute! Lisa Schubert. Archibald McNaughton. You're Lucky Lisa, right? You found a pailful of gold nuggets yesterday out at the Wattie-McNaughton place. Well, I never! Who'd a thought you're nobbut a girl?" He stared at me with his mouth open.

"It was one nugget," I said stiffly, "not a pailful, only one."

The postmaster didn't pay any attention. I could see he hadn't heard anything I had said. A woman entered, setting the bell over the door to ringing. What a sight she was: a miner's red flannel shirt, a man's felt hat, and a skirt that had certainly started life as flour sacks, though the printing on them had faded from wear and washing. "Afternoon, Mr. Harkness, anything for me?"

"One letter, from the court, Miss Ord," said the postmaster. He handed a big envelope over the counter. I could see the red wax seal that kept it closed. "Here," he went on, "allow me to introduce Lucky Lisa, Miss Ord, one mining woman to another. This little gal found herself a bucketful of gold the day after she got here. How's that for luck? Lisa Schubert, meet Miss Eliza Ord."

"Miss Schubert," Miss Ord nodded politely. "I wish you well in keeping whatever you may find or earn. Don't let anybody call you mad or crazy or insane."

I couldn't help staring at her. Did anyone ever have a stranger conversation?

"I don't understand you, ma'am," I said.

"That's what they called me," she said. "They sent me to the madhouse in New Westminster and jumped my claims and junked my boarding house while I was gone. Do I look mad to you?" She glared at me.

So this was Eliza what's-her-name. Truth to tell, she did look as crazy as anyone I'd ever seen. Her eyes burned hot enough to start a grass fire in the prairie. "N-no, ma'am," I replied.

"Miss Schubert," Miss Ord nodded politely. "I wish you well in keeping whatever you may find or earn. Don't let anybody call you mad or crazy or insane."

"Hmph," she snorted. "That's what the doctors at the madhouse said, that I was perfectly sane. Jealous idiots, those *men;* they tried to get rid of me, but I came back. Sue them all, that's what I say, and that's what I'm doing, starting with that Constable Lindsay who dragged me down to NewWest. If you've got a bucketful of gold, you can buy half of my claim."

"Buy half of your lawsuit, you mean," said the postmaster. "You ain't got a claim any more, Miss Ord."

"That's for the court to say." She waved her letter with the red seal at me and stamped out of the building. The door slammed behind her.

"She sure talks crazy," said the postmaster. "Them doctors haven't seen as much of her as we have here. Take my advice, Miss Lisa, and don't you have nothing to do with her."

I sidled toward the door again, wishing I had left before Miss Eliza Ord had entered—but meeting her had been an adventure, all the same, and I could hardly wait to tell Archie and

Mrs. Mac. Meanwhile, where would I find the Hudson's Bay Company trading post or any kind of general store?

Taylor's Drug Store was next on my route, with Mr. Lewis's barber shop, dentist office, and bathhouse on the other side of the same building. Mr. Lewis's sign said he would "fill teeth with gold, silver, or tinfoil, set teeth on pivots, repair plates, and extract teeth." There was no dentist in Kamloops; Papa should come here to get his toothache fixed. Next was a brewery advertising Triple X Ale, then the Masonic Hall. Next was Colin McCallum's tailor shop.

Was that Mr. McCallum from the Overlanders' trek? I wasn't sure of his first name, but Colin sounded right. If so, I knew him. I didn't stop, however, because the next building, at last, after a stretch of vacant land, was the Hudson's Bay Company Store, where I bought Mrs. Mac's writing paper. I thanked the clerk but did not say who I was. I didn't want anybody else staring at me and calling me Lucky Lisa.

CHAPTER № 5

My adventures for the day were not yet over. As I walked home, two of the ladies from the Occidental Hotel came toward me. Fraulein Greta was one of them. The two ladies tried to hold their skirts out of the mud, but they were draggled at the edges all the same.

Fraulein Greta nodded to me and then asked, "How you know Sammy Stokes?"

"Mr. Stokes is a partner in a mine," I said. "I live with Mr. and Mrs. McNaughton. Mr. McNaughton is a partner too."

"Rich man," said Fraulein Greta. "He ask me

to marry him."

"Rich man?" I was confused. "Mr. Stokes? He's not rich."

"Rich man," she said again. "Maybe I marry him."

Grown-ups should learn to listen. I could tell Fraulein Greta a few things about Mr. Samuel Stokes, but it didn't seem as if it would be any use. I shook my head and we all went on our way. My head was in a whirl: The postmaster, Miss Eliza Ord, Fraulein Greta and the other ladies, Mrs. Mac's leg that she hurt—and Mr. Samuel Stokes.

When I got home, Archie was there. He had made tea and cut some of my fresh bread. The room still had that wonderful smell of baking, and I was hungry. I was on my second slice of bread and dripping before we began to talk.

"So, what did you see, Lisa?" asked Mrs. Mac. "What do you think of this town?"

Archie grinned at me. "I bet you had some adventures," he said.

I told them about Miss Eliza Ord. "She looked strange," I said. "Her skirt was made from old flour sacks."

"Don't judge a man by his clothes," said Mrs. Mac. "Or a woman either. Maybe she has no money for better."

"That's true," said Archie. "She's spent every penny, I believe."

"Is it true?" I asked. "Did some men here really send her to the madhouse and jump her claim?"

"You should call it the insane asylum," said Mrs. Mac, "not the madhouse, Lisa. That's vulgar. Archie, did it happen?"

"That's her story," said Archie uncomfortably. "If it's true, it's really nasty. Men should protect women, not take advantage of them."

"The way you have protected me," said Mrs. Mac gently. "But what if a woman has no man to protect her?"

Archie looked alarmed. "The law should protect her."

"Constable Lindsay took her to the mad—I

mean the asylum," I said. "She is suing him."

"Bad idea," said Archie.

"You mean she shouldn't do anything?" I couldn't believe it.

"Not make an open fight of it," said Archie. "You know what I mean, my dear."

"Oh yes," said Mrs. Mac. "She should talk to one or two of the powerful men, the decent ones. Better still, she should talk to their wives, get them to talk to the men. That's how it works, Lisa." She shrugged angrily. "Mr. McNaughton," she said, "this is no fit conversation for a child's ears." Archie nodded. "Lisa," Mrs. Mac continued, "let's say no more about Miss Ord. Don't worry about her. Don't think about her any more. Mr. McNaughton, my dear, it would please me very much if you would look into this matter and see if there is anything that should be done." She smiled brilliantly at Archie.

"Certainly, my love," he replied. "But we have other matters to discuss. Lisa, I've talked with my partners, and this is what we propose. For the rest of July, we'll dig and tunnel and crush rock. We'll leave the question of your nugget while we do that. Let tempers settle."

"It will be hard to wait," I said, "but I'll do my best. Mr. Ross says I can get into places too small for a man. I'll find more gold, and you and your partners will share it. Maybe you'll share some with me." Then I thought of Mr. Stokes. I didn't want to find gold for him!

"No," Mrs. Mac and Archie said at the same time. Mrs. Mac made a sign to her husband to go on. "There is plenty for you to do at home and in town with Mrs. McNaughton," he said. "I don't want to worry about either of you. Lisa, you must promise me you will not come to the mine."

I stared from one to the other. "You and I will set out to make friends with some people here," said Mrs. Mac. "It is our duty to bring civilization to the wilderness. 'Do noble deeds, not dream them all day long,' as one of the poets says. I wonder if anyone has started a library or an amateur dramatic society? You spoke of building a hospital, my dear. Who is raising funds for it?"

"Mr. Wattie is chairman of the committee." Archie smiled. "I know he will be pleased to have your help. Lisa's too."

CHAPTER No. 6

Time passed slowly as the month went on. July was unusually hot, we were told. It would have been cooler underground, but I stayed away from the mine, as Archie had demanded. Much as I wanted to be there, I did not want to see Mr. Samuel Stokes.

Mrs. Mac and I met the smelling-salts lady from the Occidental Hotel one day in the street. I tried to introduce her. Mrs. Mac held out the fingertips of her white-gloved hand. I had not seen her look down her nose like that for a long time. The smelling-salts lady's name turned out to be Fraulein Lili. "Pleased to meet you, ma'am," she told Mrs. Mac.

"Charmed," said Mrs. Mac dryly.

Then, of course, Mrs. Mac had to know how I came to know these ladies, who were "direct from Baden-Baden," as Fraulein Lili said.

"Dancing girls, I believe," she told Archie at supper that night. "I was mortified. Lisa has made some very unfortunate acquaintances in this town."

"Mr. Samuel Stokes is the most unfortunate," I said crossly, "and I did not ask to meet him."

"I think you must be talking about the Hurdy Gurdy Girls," said Archie. "Some of them lived in San Francisco for years, although they came from Germany before that."

"Do you know them well?" Mrs. Mac bit off each word angrily.

"Not well, dear wife," said Archie. "When there are hundreds of men, though, and very few women, we are glad of the few who do come. The Hurdy Gurdies appear at the Fashion Saloon every evening. Men pay to dance with them. They are not ladies, but they are decent women. Many of them marry miners. Then, of course, they don't dance any more, so they write to girls they know in Germany that this is a good place to find a husband."

"Mr. Stokes asked Fraulein Greta to marry him," I said. "He told her he was rich."

Mrs. Mac shook her head. "Lisa, I should have known a gold rush town would not be a suitable place for a young lady. There are no other girls to be your friends. I can't keep you with me every minute, and I cannot expect to find an old head on your young shoulders. I have failed in my duty to you. Mr. McNaughton, my dear, we must arrange for Lisa to go back to her family."

I howled. There is no other word to describe the noise I made. "No, no, no," I sobbed. I could not stop myself. Was this the end to all my dreams? I was to be sent home in disgrace. Ma and Papa would be ashamed of me. Gus would never stop teasing me. I think Mrs. Mac said something. Maybe Archie said something. Their voices sounded a long way away. There was a roaring sound in my ears. Much later, Mrs. Mac put an arm around me and half-led, half-carried me up to bed.

Things were better in the morning. Mrs.
Mac agreed to postpone my departure at least
until after Mr. John "Cariboo" Cameron's chris-
tening party for our town. It was to take place on
July 18, more than a week away. Then a letter
arrived from Ma telling us that the family was
moving to Lillooet and that Papa Schubert
planned to try his luck at prospecting for gold.
We might see him before the end of summer.

"Ma will be busy with the move," I pointed out.
"This is a bad time for her to be worrying about
me. And I will be good, Mrs. Mac. I promise."

Mrs. Mac laughed. "I want to do what's best for you," she said. "My problem is to decide what that may be. Let's try again, Lisa. I would miss your company."

"Me too," I said, surprised to find myself saying that and even more surprised to know I really meant it.

When I put on the brown silk dress Ma had cut down for me, it was tight across my bust, and the waist was at least an inch too high. "I thought you were growing," said Mrs. Mac. "We'll have to find a seamstress, Lisa, won't we?"

She shook her head when I told her I could sew a straight seam. We went to see Mr. McCallum at his tailor shop, and he sent Mrs. Fanny Dow to our house. Mrs. Mac dug into her trunk to find a dress made of pale blue muslin embroidered with yellow roses. "Can you cut it down for Lisa?" she asked.

Mrs. Dow stood me on a chair while she fitted and pinned. "I'll leave wide seams," she said. "You can let it out when Lisa grows."

I had never seen such a pretty dress. It had wide pagoda sleeves, and the bodice and waist were trimmed with braid. The full skirt and the neck were ruffled in white lace. Mrs. Dow made an underskirt with four hoops, not too wide, and I had to admit it was just right for the dress. She also made a huge blue muslin bow for my straw bonnet. Mrs. Mac found a pair of white kid boots that she said were too small for her, with a row of buttons at the side. We only had to stuff a little paper in the toes to make them fit. I was so excited that I made a poor job of thanking her, but I think she knew anyhow.

On the day of the party, Archie wore his kilt. The claymore that his great-great-grandfather had fought with at the battle of Culloden hung at his side. Archie said anybody with even a drop of Scottish blood should be angry because Bonnie Prince Charlie had lost at Culloden. He should have been the king of Scotland and England. Mrs. Mac said she had plenty of Scottish blood, but she wasn't going to stay angry because of a battle more than a hundred years ago, and Bonnie Prince Charlie had run away at the end of it. I didn't have any Scottish blood, but I liked Archie's big sword, though it was much too heavy for me.

Mrs. Mac was still in half-mourning for her family, who had all died of the fever in Montreal. She wore lavender silk, with tiny pearl buttons from neck to waist and more buttons to fasten each sleeve. I helped to brush her hair and to fasten it with tortoiseshell combs in loops over her ears.

"One more thing," she said and brought out a parasol for each of us, made to match our dresses.

"Ooooh!" I took a long breath. We had no cheval glass, but I stared at my reflection in the hand mirror. "I like getting dressed up like a lady," I admitted, "except I'll be scared to eat or drink anything in case I spill it."

"I'm proud of both my ladies," said Archie. He offered each of us an arm.

Everybody at the party was dressed in their Sunday best, but nobody else had matching parasols, not even Mrs. Richard Cameron, who was the hostess, since Mr. Cariboo Cameron's wife, Sophia, had died last winter. Mr. Cameron had had a giant flag made specially. Somebody said it cost five hundred dollars! A flagpole towered above us.

"Now, I call on my friend and our distinguished guest, Judge Matthew Begbie, to dedicate this flag and name our town," said Mr. Cameron.

Judge Begbie was the biggest man I had ever seen. Mr. Stokes had called him the hanging judge! My knees trembled. Mrs. Mac bent and asked in a whisper if I was feeling faint. I shook my head.

Judge Begbie's big voice rolled out over the crowd. "I hereby dedicate this flag, our Union Jack, proud symbol of the British Empire and our Sovereign Queen and Empress, and I name this town Cameronton. God bless the Queen." His huge hands pulled on the rope and slowly the flag rose up the pole. As if on cue, a breeze began to blow, just enough to fly the flag.

There was a drum roll, and a band played "God Save the Queen." We all sang heartily, even me. Then we joined a line to shake hands with our hosts and meet the judge. I still felt nervous, but I hadn't really believed what Mr. Stokes had said before, and I didn't believe it now. Not really. My hands felt sweaty inside my gloves, all the same. The line moved quickly, and soon an official was presenting Mr. Archibald McNaughton, from Montreal, Overland to Cariboo, and Archie was shaking Cariboo Cameron's hand and presenting, "My wife, also from Montreal, and our young friend, Miss Lisa Schubert, another Overlander." Mr. Cameron was saying, "Lucky Lisa, isn't it? A pleasure, Mrs. McNaughton, Miss Schubert." To the judge he said, "Your Honour, Miss Schubert found a large gold nugget on her very first day here in town. What do you think of that?"

Judge Begbie bent his great height to bow over my hand, just as he had with Mrs. McNaughton. "A pleasure, Miss Schubert," his voice boomed.

"Your Honour," I began and stopped.

*Judge Begbie bent his
great height to bow over my
hand, just as he had with
Mrs. McNaughton. "A pleasure,
Miss Schubert," his
voice boomed.*

"Yes, Miss Schubert?" His grey eyes were stern but kind.

I gulped. "Did you ever hang a young person, a girl my age?" Judge Begbie stared down at me. "I-I beg your pardon," I stammered. "I did not mean to be impertinent."

He paused, considering. "No, Miss Schubert, I believe that hanging is a punishment reserved for the most evil human beings. I have not ever tried a young woman so wicked as to deserve it. Do I relieve your mind?"

"You do indeed," I said fervently. "Thank you, Your Honour." I followed Mrs. Mac's stiff back toward the refreshment table.

"Have I disgraced you, ma'am?" I asked, in a very small voice.

She turned. "You have not," she told me, "so long as the judge does not think that I or Mr. McNaughton has frightened you with tales of hanging."

"Oh no," I said, "that was Mr. Stokes, but I didn't believe him."

"Mr. Stokes again," said Archie. "I must have another word with James Wattie. He and I hope soon to end our association with Mr. Stokes."

"I haven't asked," I said, "but I hope you have found more gold."

Archie smiled. "You have been surprisingly patient, Lisa," he said. "I have noticed. We are recovering some gold after crushing the ore, enough to cover expenses and a little bit over, but we are not taking out gold by the pailful, like Cariboo Cameron is. All the men I brought here have left us to work for him. We can't pay them what he does, ten dollars a day. Now it's just us partners working our claims, same as before. I won't have you at the mine while Samuel is still around, but soon I hope both my ladies can be out there, cheering us on."

Most of the miners did not go to church.
Mrs. Mac was shocked, and so was I, when we
found that Sunday was the biggest day of the week
for the saloons and the worst day for drunken men
staggering around the streets. I had been to many
different kinds of services on our long journey
overland from Fort Garry, sometimes conducted
by a preacher but more often by our leader,
Mr. Thomas McMicking. Mrs. Mac and Archie
were Presbyterian, but there was no Presbyterian
minister in Cameronton, or in Barkerville or
Richfield either. Reverend Sheepshanks had just

built a little log building for Anglican services in Richfield. Father Grandidier, the priest we met on our journey to the Cariboo, said mass in Richfield also.

"Ma was brought up Catholic," I told Mrs. Mac, "but we heard all kinds of preachers on our journey, missionaries mostly. Ma and Papa won't fuss about what church I go to."

"That's good," said Archie, "because Reverend Evans and Reverend Browning are building a church here in Cameronton. It's Methodist, but I'm sure we'll be welcome there."

On the Sunday after Mr. Cariboo Cameron's party, Reverend Evans read the banns of marriage for Mr. Samuel Stokes, miner, of Cameronton, and Miss Greta Mann, spinster, of the same place, the first time of asking.

Mrs. Mac tut-tutted under her breath. I had heard banns read before, but I wasn't sure what it meant; of course, I had to wait until after church to ask. "The minister has to read the banns three times, on three different Sundays," Mrs. Mac told me. "Then the people can get married. That is, if nobody comes forward to object."

"I object," I said. "Mr. Stokes is ugly, mean, and miserable and a liar besides."

"True enough." Archie tried to hide his smile.

"It's not funny," I said.

"You're right, Lisa. It's not funny," he agreed. "I'm afraid those are not reasons why he cannot get married, though. Mr. Wattie and I want to buy out his interest in our company, but he wants more money than we can offer and more than his claim is worth."

"Is my nugget enough?" I asked.

"No," he said. "Though it would be a big help, Lisa. Do you want to buy his claim?"

"Yes, I do," I said. "Then I'll get to share our gold, won't I?"

"You will," Archie agreed.

"Can't you stop him from marrying Fraulein Greta?" I asked.

"I don't think so," said Archie. "He says he has never been married. He and the lady are certainly old enough. He may have lied about being rich, but it's not for us to object if Miss Mann does not. Well, this is only the first time of asking. Something may happen before the three weeks have passed. Meanwhile, Lisa, Mr. and Mrs. Kelly will take Sunday tea with us this afternoon and Miss Eliza Ord as well. Perhaps we can help her."

"Do the Kellys own the Wake-Up Jake?" I asked, a huge grin spreading over my face. "That's the funniest name for a restaurant."

"Sure is." Archie grinned too and so did Mrs. Mac. "D'you know how it got its name? Jake McGregor, foreman at Cariboo Cameron's mine and deaf as a doornail, always eats there. Every night after supper, he puts his head down on the table and goes to sleep. When it's time to close, Mr. Kelly shakes him and yells in his ear, 'Wake up, Jake!' Everybody laughs. It's a good name, isn't it?"

"They seem like decent people," said Mrs. Mac. "Mr. Kelly opened a bakery first, they tell me, and he owns other businesses as well."

I wanted to talk to the Hurdy Gurdies. If Fraulein Greta did not understand what I had tried to tell her about Mr. Stokes, maybe Fraulein Lili would listen. However, Sunday was not a good day to go to the Occidental Hotel, even if I had been able to think of an excuse. Besides, I did not want to miss the tea party. Somehow, I was certain that Archie would let me stay with the grown-ups, even if Mrs. Mac did not exactly approve.

"You have certainly been badly treated," said Mrs. Kelly later to Miss Ord, setting down her delicate teacup with a thump.

"Has any gold been taken from your claim?" asked Mr. Kelly.

Miss Ord shook her head. "Seems there's no gold on it at all," she said grumpily. "I might've sold it, though, and kept on looking. I've got no money to sue them, let alone that Stokes fellow they're living with. He likely put them up to the whole thing."

"Samuel Stokes?" Archie asked sharply.

"Samuel Stokes." Miss Ord bared her rather yellow teeth. "He's one of the men who swore the complaint about me."

"Did you provoke him?" Mrs. Mac looked straight at the angry woman.

Miss Ord laughed. "I broke all the windows in James Bruce's house," she said. "James owed me board money, and he refused to pay. I said I'd make him sorry, and I did. He went to court and swore I was mad, and Sam Stokes backed him up. That's when Constable Lindsay took me off to the madhouse. Didn't take the doctors long to say I was as sane as them, but there I was in New Westminster with no money. It took me a while to get back, and by then everything was gone, even my pickaxe and my pans."

"What do you want to do, Miss Ord?" asked Mr. Kelly. "Mrs. Kelly and I will outfit you, if you want to go prospecting. You've panned for gold before, and there are still streams where you can make a decent wage."

"The Chinamen have taken over the streams," said Miss Ord. "I'd have to go a far piece, and soon it will be too late for this season. Much obliged, I'm sure, but that's not for me. Help me to sue the thieves, if you'd be so kind. The judge who sent me to that madhouse was a lily-livered fool, but Matthew Begbie is a different kind of man. He won't let them get away with it."

"Mr. Stokes doesn't have any money," I said. "How about Mr. James Bruce?"

"He left town after I came back," said Miss Ord. "He didn't wait around." Her eyes shone. I could see what she wanted: a fight.

"Miss Ord, I fear there is little we can do for you," said Mrs. Mac gently. "If I might advise you to be less quarrelsome, your life would be easier."

Miss Ord stood abruptly, smoothing her flour-sack skirts. "That's as may be, ma'am," she said.

"You don't know what it's like for a woman on her own."

"I don't," Mrs. Mac agreed. "Lisa, please show Miss Ord to the door."

"I'm sorry, Miss Ord," I said, holding the door open for her. "I thought you wanted to go mining again. I thought it would be a noble deed to help you."

"Don't you worry about me, child," she said. "I can cook—that'll get me through the winter—and I can get a grubstake to go mining next year, if I want. You go find somebody else that needs a noble deed worse than me."

CHAPTER N°. 9

It's hard, trying to help somebody who won't let you. Mr. and Mrs. Kelly said they would talk to Constable Lindsay and ask him to apologize and they would ask Miss Ord to drop her lawsuit against him, and that was that.

The next Sunday, the banns for Mr. Samuel Stokes and Miss Greta Mann were read for the second time. I still had not talked to Fraulein Lili. Fraulein Greta did not know what Miss Ord had told us about Samuel Stokes. I decided to ask Archie to come for a walk with me. I wouldn't go alone to a hotel on Sunday, but I would be safe with Archie. I hoped he would go along with my plan.

It looked as if all the miners were out drinking, and lots of them were already staggering around. Archie took my arm as we walked. His mouth set hard. "I won't keep this secret from Mrs. McNaughton," he said. "However, Lisa, you know things far beyond your years. This is not exactly a good thing," he added, looking around grimly, "but it is a fact. Mrs. McNaughton has not crossed prairies, swamps, and mountains. She has not rafted down a wild river, saved herself and her brother from drowning, almost starved, or helped to birth a baby. You have. She does not know the Hurdy Gurdies and thinks worse of them than they deserve. So I will meet those ladies with you. I will let you have your say. Afterward, Lisa, you must tell Mrs. McNaughton everything. Do you agree?"

I thought of telling Mrs. McNaughton I had deceived her. I could almost hear her telling me she had failed again in her duty. I could see the sad look in her eyes. I started to turn around and march back home. Then I thought about Fraulein Greta and Mr. Stokes and told Archie, in a very small voice, that I agreed.

"It won't be as bad as you think," he said.

First, however, I had a lot of explaining to do. It was easy enough to find Fraulein Lili and Fraulein Greta. They were sitting with some other Hurdy Gurdy ladies on the porch at the Occidental Hotel. Some miners were talking to the ladies, but Fraulein Lili and Fraulein Greta walked down the steps to meet us, their huge skirts swaying. We all walked to a little space with benches and a few straggly roses struggling to climb a trellis. Maybe some day, it would be a garden. Meanwhile, it was a place to sit, with nobody else nearby.

How do you tell a grown-up that her friend shouldn't marry somebody—especially when the friend is sitting right there and next week the banns will be read for the third time? *Oh dear,* I thought, *I do get myself into trouble.* But I knew Mr. Stokes was a liar and a cheat. How could

Fraulein Greta want to marry him? If I told her the truth, that would surely be a noble deed. So I took a deep breath and came right out with it.

"I think Mr. Stokes has been fooling Fraulein Greta," I said. "He is a nasty man. I can't prove it, but I'm sure he put a dead raccoon outside our door for Mrs. McNaughton to trip over. He and his friend Mr. Bruce swore that Miss Eliza Ord was mad; they told lies to the judge so that he would send her to the insane asylum at New Westminster. Not Judge Begbie," I added, "another judge."

Fraulein Lili raised her eyebrows.

"Miss Greta asked me if Samuel Stokes is rich," I hurried on. "I don't believe he is. Mr. McNaughton doesn't believe Mr. Stokes is rich either."

Fraulein Greta started talking in German to Fraulein Lili, and the two spoke back and forth for a long time. At last Fraulein Lili turned to me.

"Miss Greta does not talk English so good," she said, "but she understands plenty. Mr. Stokes says he

is rich. He wants to buy some claims from his partners. Six claims. He says they are rich claims, but his
partners don't know that. He must buy soon,
before they know. Greta has give him some money
already. Me too but not so much. We Hurdy
Gurdies work hard and save, save. Start business, get
married." She shrugged her shoulders. "Miss Greta
and me, we are getting old." She laughed.

"You're not old," I said. But then I looked up
at her, forgetting to be polite. She had wrinkle
lines like Ma's around her nose and eyes. Fraulein
Greta put her hand over mine. I could see the
ropey blue veins in it.

"Pretty old for dancing," said Fraulein Lili.
"Plenty of young girls dance. For me and Greta,
it comes time to get married. I go south this
winter, and I won't come back. Marry some
farmer, get me plenty Holstein cows for milking.
But Greta, she wants satin dresses and rubies and
diamonds like Mrs. Billy Barker. Samuel Stokes
say he buy them for her. He gives her one nugget
already. Here, Greta, let them see."

She pointed to Greta's pocket, and Greta took out a little wash leather bag, tied with a drawstring. She opened the bag and shook three nuggets into her left hand. Greta pointed to one almost as big as my nugget. "That one," she said. The gold shone softly in the afternoon sun.

Archie's eyebrows went up. "Mr. Stokes has lied to you," he said, "and to us as well. I am one of his partners. We would never sell to him. If this nugget came from our claims, it was not his to give."

I could see from her face that Fraulein Greta understood him perfectly. Before she could say anything, however, a voice sounded behind us. "Ladies, Greta, my love."

I knew that voice. Mr. Stokes! The three nuggets vanished into Fraulein Greta's pouch, and the pouch into her pocket, as I turned.

"Snoopy Schubert, what are you doing here?" he hissed. His hand clenched and his fist shot toward my ear. I ducked fast but not fast enough to dodge the blow completely. He caught the side of my head. Ma has sometimes paddled me but only when I deserved it. Nobody has ever hit my head. They say you see stars, and I did. I was so dizzy, I almost fell.

Luckily, I did not lose my senses. I will never forget what happened next. Fraulein Greta knew a thing or two about fighting and so did Fraulein Lili, as it turned out. The ladies had given Mr. Stokes two black eyes and a scratched face before Archie could get to his feet. Mr. Stokes backed away from us. Fraulein Greta picked up a rock and threw it. She hit him on the shin, and he yelped.

"Go," said Greta furiously. "Go. Come back, my money bring. I not marry you."

"Bring my money too," said Fraulein Lili. Both ladies picked up more stones. Mr. Stokes backed away from us. He tripped over a rock and fell. The ladies laughed at him. Archie did too. I did not laugh. Mr. Stokes's face had turned purple with rage. He got up and stamped away, his feet thumping like blows on the ground.

CHAPTER N° 10

I told Mrs. Mac everything. Archie was right; it was not as hard as I had expected, especially since Fraulein Greta was not going to marry Mr. Stokes after all.

"I don't like the way you went about it," Mrs. Mac told me. "Don't go behind my back again, Lisa. And don't you encourage her, Mr. McNaughton." She glared at Archie. Then she smiled at both of us. "You are right, though, Lisa, it was a noble deed."

"He talked of buying out his partners," Archie said. "It's time for us to buy him out instead."

"Can we use my nugget?" I asked.

"Yes," said Archie. "You can't use it to bring your family here, though, if we do that."

"Of course not," I said. "But I want to be partners with you." I smiled inside. I could use my share of the gold we would find for my family.

"You would be a partner," he agreed. "One nugget would not be enough, especially if our friend Samuel has found more gold on our property. But I expect he'll settle fast enough if there's money to pay his debts and enough over for him to go somewhere else."

It turned out that Mr. Stokes had no money, except a little left from what Fraulein Greta had lent him. He could not pay her back. He owed money to four other Hurdy Gurdies, as well as to the Kellys for bread and whiskey and to the outfitters for mining gear. Other folk lined up to try to collect more money that he owed.

I needed more money to buy my claim. Fraulein Greta gave me her smallest nugget and lent me the rest. Fraulein Lili explained why.

"Greta would not have any money if she had married Mr. Stokes. Her husband would have everything, at least to use, her money as well as his own. She would have to pay off his debts. You saved her, Lisa."

"Is that true?" I stared at Mrs. Mac and Archie. Mrs. Mac had finally met Fraulein Lili and Fraulein Greta properly. This was the second time she had invited them to tea, since I had business with Fraulein Greta. Mrs. Mac still did not want me to spend much time with them though.

"It's true," said Mrs. Mac. "A single woman with money must be very careful whom she marries. Very careful indeed." She gave Archie one of her loving looks.

"That's terrible," I said. "That's as bad as having slaves, and they had a war in America so the slaves would be free. We haven't had slaves here for a long time, I know that."

"I'm not a slave, am I?" said Mrs. Mac. "Your ma is not a slave, nor is Mrs. Kelly. Some women think the law should be changed, and maybe some day it will be. Meanwhile, it is a man's duty to protect his wife and to provide for her and for their children. That's what good men do."

"I'm not getting married," I said. "Not ever. Archie, can I go mining now?"

We had a meeting of all the partners. Mrs. Mac was there as well. Archie had made over one of his claims to her. It did not make much difference, as far as I could see. He was still her husband, and he could decide everything. But I knew he would talk to his wife and not do things she did not like—at least he'd try, just like Papa did.

It was not much different for me. I owned Mr. Stokes's claim now, but Archie and James Wattie would decide everything. I did get to choose, though, whether Archie and Mr. Wattie together or Papa Schubert would look after my claim. That was a hard choice, but Archie and Mr. Wattie knew more about mining, and they were here, so I chose them.

They both said I could go down into the mine, though there was only room for two people at a time. I have gone down twice so far. It is wet and dark, even with a lantern, and I did not find any gold. We were also looking to see if Mr. Stokes had been digging anywhere else on our property, but we had not found anything. Not yet.

CHAPTER N.º 11

Water started coming into our mine. Archie and the others had to stop digging while they built a Cornish Wheel to take it out and a flume to carry it away. They built a sluice so that they could use the water to wash the gold out of the crushed rock. There was not a lot of gold, just little bits and some dust.

While they worked, I kept trying to find where Mr. Stokes had been digging, if he had been digging on our property at all. I looked for another shaft like the one we were digging. I hammered posts into the ground so I'd know where I had already looked. July turned into August, and then August was half over. Most days were still warm, but the nights were getting colder. Winter came early in the Cariboo.

I usually came back to the mine in the afternoon and sat with my partners while we had our tea.

"I think I've been everywhere," I said one day. "If Mr. Stokes was digging, there would have to be a pile of dirt, as well as a shaft. I could not have missed it."

"Maybe it's not a shaft," Mr. Wattie said suddenly. He looked up. "I should have thought of this before. Maybe it's an adit."

"An adit?" I had never heard the word.

"An opening into the side of a hill," said Mr. Wattie. He looked at me impatiently. "A shaft goes up and down, right?" I nodded. "An adit goes sideways. The entrance could be a crack in the rock, just big enough to squeeze through. There could be a cave inside, big enough for a miner to pile up dirt and rock from his digging where nobody would see it." He shook his head. "I wish I'd thought of this sooner, Lisa."

I jumped up. "Ouch!" My hot tea spilled onto my dirty skirt.

"Can't you wait until tomorrow?" Archie laughed. I laughed too.

"It won't be easy," I said, "but I can wait."

I ran all the way home. While I helped Mrs. Mac with supper, I told her about adits. Then she told me she had gone to the post office that afternoon and had brought back a letter for me.

"Papa is coming!" I said, reading the letter quickly. "He will be here before the end of August."

"That's very late for prospecting," said Archie later, as we ate our pie. "He'd better have waited until next season. You'll be glad to see him though, Lisa, and so will I."

"If he goes back to Lillooet for the winter," said Mrs. Mac, "you may want to go with him. We would miss you, Lisa, but it is something to think about."

"Bad timing," Archie chuckled, looking at me.

"I have to look for an adit," I said. "I can't go now."

CHAPTER N° 12

An opening in the side of a hill, that's what I was looking for. There were plenty of places it could be. It would not be easy to find, or I would have seen something already. Maybe not, though. I had not gone into every little thicket. I had not climbed onto every ledge.

This time I had to look everywhere. Mr. Wattie gave me a lantern and a flint to light it. He gave me a rope to wrap around my waist. "I know you, Lisa," he said. "I don't want you going into a dark place and getting scared, or lost maybe. If you find the kind of place we're looking for, tie your rope to something at the entrance, and light your lantern. You'll see soon enough if Sam Stokes was there, and if he was, Lisa, you come right along and get us. That's an order."

"Yes, Mr. Wattie," I said.

It was late in August before I found it, just a little crack in a rocky hill. Brambles covered the opening, and I would not have gone near except that the prickly bushes looked more dried out than the others around. I pulled them aside, ignoring my scratched arms, and pushed into the opening. It was easy enough for me, though it would have been a tight squeeze for a man, even a small man like Mr. Stokes. But I was sure, right then, that this was the place.

My hands trembled with excitement as I struck my flint. It took three tries to light the lantern. I tied my rope around a rock and let the rope out as I went. The crack opened into a cave, and there was a pile of rock and mud. A pickaxe leaned against the pile, with a spade and a wooden bucket beside it.

Maybe Mr. Stokes had only pretended to leave the Cariboo. Maybe he had come back already. If not, surely he would come back soon. I had to see what he had found. I held up the lantern, looking for a passage leading out of the cave, the adit. The first tunnel went for six paces and then I came to solid rock. The next tunnel ended too, but it ended in a pile of stones and dirt. Was it a cave-in? Could I climb over it? I held up my lantern but I couldn't see over the heap. Then I began to climb up on the pile. The rocks were wet and slippery, but soon I was pretty sure they did not go all the way to the top of the tunnel.

In my head, I could hear Mr. Wattie telling me to go and get him and the others. "That's an order," he had said.

Yes, but he had not exactly said I couldn't look around first. I'd feel pretty silly if I went off and fetched everybody and there was nothing to find. And if there *was* something, I wanted to find it first. I would be careful, and I was light. That was the show-off part of me, not common sense. If rocks fell and trapped me, I could be a skeleton before anybody found me, if they ever did.

Then I stopped thinking about danger. I had to hold the lantern carefully. I had to climb over that wet dirt pile without my rope getting tangled up. A few rocks fell as I slithered down the other side, but that was all. There was a tiny pool of light around me from the lantern, fading quickly into darkness, the blackest dark I had ever been in. The walls seemed to press in as I went forward; indeed, after a few steps, I could see, and feel, rock on both sides of me. My ball of rope had been getting smaller and smaller. Where it ended, I made a little pile of rocks to mark the place. Then I walked slowly forward. I could hear water dripping not far away. I held the lantern to one wall, then the other, but there wasn't the slightest glint of gold, not even fool's gold, just dark rock. I could not be sure that Mr. Stokes had ever climbed over the rock pile. Soon the passage was too narrow for any grown-up, and then too narrow even for me.

Now I felt gloomily certain that there was no gold here. Maybe the pickaxe and the other things did not belong to Mr. Stokes at all. Maybe some other miner had left them here. Maybe the rock pile had fallen and killed him, and I would trip over his dead hand when I tried to climb over the rocks on my way back.

I began to run. I tripped over a rock and would have fallen if the wall had not been so close. The lantern almost fell, but I managed to hold onto it. Then I had to sit down for a minute because my legs felt funny. I set the lantern very carefully on the ground.

And there, on the ground beside the lantern, I saw blue clay, and—was it really?—something glittering.

I scratched at the clay with my fingernails and dug at it with the button hook from my pocket. I had no knife, and I had left the spade where I found it. There it was, though, a nugget, bigger than my first one. It went into my pocket. I moved the lantern and scratched again in the clay until I hit something solid. It took ages to scrape off the dirt, and then all I saw was a big dark rock. I worked the square toe of my boot under one side and managed to turn the rock over. There again was gold, a little seam of it. There might be lots more. Finding one nugget, or two or three, was not nearly as good as finding a seam, like a tiny river of gold. The rock was too heavy for me to carry. I would have to lead the others to it.

I picked up my lantern and shook it gently. It felt light. There was a little oil left but not much. I'd have to hurry. What if my light went out? I was not careful on my way back. I wanted to run and yell and jump up and down. Then I saw my rock pile and grabbed the end of my rope. A few more rocks fell as I climbed over the cave-in, but they didn't hurt me. I was lucky. The lantern went out, but not before I saw the sun, low in the sky, beyond the cave.

*And there, on the ground
beside the lantern, I saw blue
clay, and—was it really?—
something glittering.*

"Hold out your hand," said Mr. Wattie.
He unbuttoned his suspenders and strapped me
three times on my right hand with the warm
leather. That was my reward for finding gold for
the second time.

It was a mean trick, but I did not say anything.
"Your turn, Archie." Mr. Wattie marched me over.
Would you believe it? Archie whipped me too.
Three times, but not as hard as Mr. Wattie did.

My hand stung. It did not hurt much, but my
pride hurt something awful. "You might've *died*
being a glory hog," Archie said thickly. "If you

can't learn one way, Lisa, you'll have to learn another. Mrs. Mac may want a turn at you too."

"Please don't tell her." My face was hot with shame. "I have learned my lesson, truly I have. I won't do anything like that again."

"We will both be watching you, Lisa," said Mr. Wattie. "If you keep your word and don't take one more dangerous chance, I think we *may* keep your secret. If Mr. McNaughton agrees, eh, Archie?"

Would Archie agree? I held my breath. At last he nodded, and his grim face relaxed a little. "Can you lead us to the place?" he asked me. "How far away is it? If the three of us go together, we can take care of each other. Perhaps we will allow Lisa to climb that rock pile and see what she can find. If you agree, James."

"Mind you, it goes sore against my conscience," said Mr. Wattie.

"Mine also," said Archie. "I will not deceive my wife, of course, but perhaps I need not tell her all the details of your discovery." He stared at me.

"Thank you," I said. "I will be careful. Believe me, I will."

Nobody said anything as I led the way. When we got to the right place, Archie squeezed through behind me. Mr. Wattie pulled in his stomach as much as he could, but the hole was too small for him. Archie widened it a little with the pickaxe.

"This entrance is part of Mrs. McNaughton's claim, I believe," said Mr. Wattie. "If we do find a seam of gold, or gold ore, it may continue onto other claims of ours. It's a good thing this discovery is not at the edge of our property. The gold-bearing ore, if there is some, might extend onto somebody else's land."

"Even if it's underground?" I asked.

"Yes," he said. "But I don't think that will happen. Nobody has found a really long seam yet here in the Cariboo."

With Archie and Mr. Wattie right there, the rock pile was hardly scary at all.

Archie let me go first. "You're the lightest," he said.

"I'll stay here," said Mr. Wattie. "I'm as heavy as both of you put together. Besides, one of us needs to stay where he won't be caught in a cave-in."

A lot of stones and mud fell when Archie clambered over the pile, but I jumped out of the way. Archie kneeled down. The seam of gold gleamed in the circle of lantern light. Archie whistled.

"Well done, Lisa," he said. "James, I think you'll like this. Best to leave it where it is, though, until we're ready to explore our new find properly. There's a nice little seam of gold, and I expect it will lead us to more."

"Discovery," said Mr. Wattie cheerfully. "Good work, partners. Lisa, you come back first. Don't hurry, we have plenty of time."

We had a party at the McNaughton home that night, just us partners. Mrs. Mac had made a huge pot of stew, with carrots and potatoes and onions, as well as cubes of beef. We decided not to tell the town about our discovery, not until we had cleared the rock pile. "We must post guards," said Mr. Wattie. "Our news will get around fast. Davie Ross, will you stand watch with me tonight?"

Mr. Ross had only just agreed when somebody knocked at the door. I could hardly keep my eyes open. It had been an amazing day, and I was very tired. I got up, however, and opened the door.

There stood Papa, blinking in the light that poured out. It was dusk by then but not full dark. Papa held out his arms, and I ran into them. I pulled down his face to kiss him. His face was whiskery. "Let me take off my glasses," he said, with the familiar laugh in his voice. "Then I can kiss my girl properly."

So he did, and we did, and Papa came into the little house, his eyes shining brighter than any nugget. A fire blazed on the hearth, and the stew still simmered on the back of the cookstove. We all started talking at once. I wasn't tired any more, listening to Papa's adventures, telling him mine. Maybe I would not sleep at all that night. Papa could stay only a few days, but at least he was here. I put my arms around him and smiled into his waistcoat. For the second time that day, I had found gold.

ACKNOWLEDGEMENTS

Many of the same sources that so richly contributed to Book Two were similarly helpful in my research for Book Three, including the Internet, my own library, and the Robarts Library at the University of Toronto. Books by Fred Ludditt, Richard Thomas Wright, Branwen C. Patenaude, and others provided splendid background detail. Family records, including photographs and letters as well as a few treasured articles from the period, helped me with authentic details of fashion, language, and home life in Lisa's time. My great-grandmother, b. 1831, travelled with her children from Port Hawkesbury in Nova Scotia to New Westminster in British Columbia. She wore a brooch of silver inlaid with a carved design in silver and gold, and she carried a sealskin purse with a silver-coloured top and a clasp that locked. The brooch and the purse, including the key, eventually came to me. My sadiron came from my second husband's collection, and my wash-board is on loan from a friend, although I owned and used one myself in the 1950s, when a washing machine was, for me, an impossible dream.

My writing group has provided support and criticism for almost twenty-five years; thanks, Ayanna, Barb, Heather, Lorraine, Pat, Sylvia, and Vancy.

Dear Reader,

*Welcome back to Our Canadian Girl!
In addition to this story about Lisa,
there are many more adventures of other
spirited girls to come.*

*So please keep on reading. And do stay
in touch. You can also log on to our website
at www.ourcanadiangirl.ca and enjoy fun
activities, sample chapters, a fan club, and
monthly contests.*

*Sincerely,
Barbara Berson
Editor*

Canada's

1608
Samuel de Champlain establishes the first fortified trading post at Quebec.

1759
The British defeat the French in the Battle of the Plains of Abraham.

1812
The United States declares war against Canada.

1845
The expedition of Sir John Franklin to the Arctic ends when the ship is frozen in the pack ice; the fate of its crew remains a mystery.

1869
Louis Riel leads his Métis followers in the Red River Rebellion.

1871
British Columbia joins Canada.

1755
The British expel the entire French population of Acadia (today's Maritime provinces), sending them into exile.

1776
The 13 Colonies revolt against Britain, and the Loyalists flee to Canada.

1762
Elizabeth

1837
Calling for responsible government, the Patriotes, following Louis-Joseph Papineau, rebel in Lower Canada; William Lyon Mackenzie leads the uprising in Upper Canada.

1867
New Brunswick, Nova Scotia, and the United Province of Canada come together in Confederation to form the Dominion of Canada.

1870
Manitoba joins Canada. The Northwest Territories become an official territory of Canada.

1863
Lisa

Timeline

1885
At Craigellachie, British Columbia, the last spike is driven to complete the building of the Canadian Pacific Railway.

1898
The Yukon Territory becomes an official territory of Canada.

1914
Britain declares war on Germany, and Canada, because of its ties to Britain, is at war too.

1918
As a result of the Wartime Elections Act, the women of Canada are given the right to vote in federal elections.

1945
World War II ends conclusively with the dropping of atomic bombs on Hiroshima and Nagasaki.

1873
Prince Edward Island joins Canada.

1896
Gold is discovered on Bonanza Creek, a tributary of the Klondike River.

1905
Alberta and Saskatchewan join Canada.

1917
In the Halifax harbour, two ships collide, causing an explosion that leaves more than 1,600 dead and 9,000 injured.

1939
Canada declares war on Germany seven days after war is declared by Britain and France.

1949
Newfoundland, under the leadership of Joey Smallwood, joins Canada.

1897
Emily

1940
Ellen

Read more about Lisa in *Overland to Cariboo* and *The Trail to Golden Cariboo*

In *Overland to Cariboo*, Lisa and her family travel across prairies, mountains, and dangerous rivers on their journey to the goldfields of British Columbia. Before reaching their destination, Lisa's parents decide to settle in Kamloops. In *The Trail to Golden Cariboo*, Lisa goes on to Cariboo with her cousin and his new wife to find gold all on her own.

OUR
CANADIAN
Girl

They're dreamers
and schemers.

They're sisters,
daughters, and friends.

Sometimes, they're
even heroes.

Meet all the *Our Canadian Girls*
at www.ourcanadiangirl.ca

Angelique   Elizabeth   Ellen   Emily

Izzie   Keeley   Lisa   Margit

Marie-Claire   Millie   Penelope   Rachel

Penguin Group (Canada)